To parents and teachers

We hope you and the children will enjoy reading this story in either English or French. The story is simple, but not *simplified* so the language of the French and the English is quite natural but there is lots of repetition.

At the back of the book is a small picture dictionary with the key words and how to pronounce them. There is also a simple pronunciation guide to the whole story on the last page.

Here are a few suggestions on using the book:

- Read the story aloud in English first, to get to know it. Treat it like any other picture book: look at the pictures, talk about the story and the characters and so on.

- Then look at the picture dictionary and say the French names for the key words. Ask the children to repeat them. Concentrate on speaking the words out loud, rather than reading them.

- Go back and read the story again, this time in English *and* French. Don't worry if your pronunciation isn't quite correct. Just have fun trying it out. Check the guide at the back of the book, if necessary, but you'll soon pick up how to say the French words.

- When you think you and the children are ready, you can try reading the story in French only. Ask the children to say it with you. Only ask them to read it if they are keen to try. The spelling could be confusing and put them off.

- Above all encourage the children to have a go and give lots of praise. Little children are usually quite unselfconscious and this is excellent for building up confidence in a foreign language.

Published by b small publishing
Pinewood, 3a Coombe Ridings, Kingston upon Thames, Surrey KT2 7JT
© **b small publishing, 2000**
1 2 3 4 5
All rights reserved.
Design: *Lone Morton*   Editorial: *Catherine Bruzzone and Olivia Norton*   Special thanks to: *Claudine Bharadia*
Production: *Grahame Griffiths and Olivia Norton*
Colour reproduction: *Vimnice International* Printed in Hong Kong by *Wing King Tong Co. Ltd.*
ISBN 1 874735 98 0 (hardback)
British Library Cataloguing in Publication Data. A catalogue record for this book is available from the British Library.

Hurry up, Molly

Dépêche-toi, Molly

Lone Morton

Pictures by Gill Scriven
French by Christophe Dillinger

"Come on Molly, into the bathroom.
Then I'll read you a story", says Dad.

"Allez Molly, dans la salle de bain.
Ensuite je te raconterai une histoire",
dit papa.

"Carry me, carry me!"
Dad picks Molly up.

"Porte-moi, porte-moi!"
Papa prend Molly dans ses bras.

"Upside down?"

"La tête en bas?"

"Over my shoulder?"
"Sur mon épaule?"

"Or on my back?" asks Dad.
"Ou sur mon dos?" demande papa.

"Like a baby!" says Molly, laughing.

"Comme un bébé!" dit Molly en riant.

"Hurry up Molly," Dad says,
"I'll wait in your bedroom."

"Dépêche-toi, Molly," dit papa,
"Je vais t'attendre dans ta chambre."

"Wash your face," he calls,
"Lave-toi la figure," crie-t-il,

"and behind your ears."
"et derrière les oreilles."

"Brush your teeth."

"Lave-toi les dents."

Molly also brushes her hair…
Molly se brosse aussi les cheveux…

to the left…
à la gauche…

…to the right,
…à la droite,

…over her nose,
…sur son nez,

and all on top of her head!
et le tout sur le haut de sa tête!

Molly looks in Dad's mirror.
Molly se regarde dans le miroir de papa.

Her chin is long,
Son menton est long,

…her eyes are big,
…ses yeux sont gros,

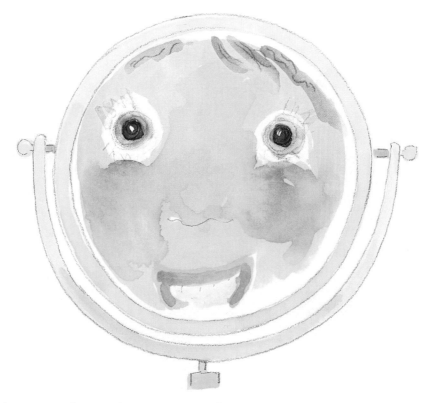

…her cheeks are fat.
…ses joues sont rondes.

What a sight!
Quel spectacle!

She puts some powder on her hand,
and blows…

Elle se met de la poudre dans la main,
et elle souffle…

…and blows!
…et elle souffle!

What a mess!
Quel désastre!

She sprays some perfume
on her neck…

Elle se met du parfum dans le cou…

…and on her toes.
…et sur ses doigts de pied.

What a smell!
Quelle odeur!

Molly suddenly remembers her Dad.
"Just coming Dad!" she calls.

Soudain, Molly se souvient de son
papa. "J'arrive papa!" crie-t-elle.

But guess what Molly finds
in her bedroom?

Mais devine ce que Molly trouve
dans sa chambre?

"Dad, wake up! I want a story!"
"Papa, réveille-toi! Je veux une histoire!"

But he's fast asleep and snoring!
Mais il dort profondement et il ronfle!

Pronouncing French

Don't worry if your pronunciation isn't quite correct.
The important thing is to be willing to try. The pronunciation guide here will help but it cannot be completely accurate:

- Read the guide as naturally as possible, as if it were standard British English.

- Put stress on the letters in *italics*, e.g. pap-*ah*.

- Don't roll the r at the end of the word, for example in the French word **le** (the): ler.

If you can, ask a French person to help and move on as soon as possible to speaking the words without the guide.

Words Les Mots

leh moh

left
à gauche

ah gosh

right
à droite

ah drwaht

hair

les cheveux

leh sher-*ver*

face

la figure

lah feeg-*yoor*

eye/eyes

l'œil/les yeux

ler-yee/lez yer

cheek

la joue

lah shoo

ears

les oreilles

leh zo*ray*

chin

le menton

ler mon*toh*

nose

le nez

ler neh

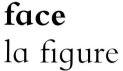

neck

le cou

ler coo

teeth

les dents

leh doh

head

la tête

lah tet

shoulder

l'épaule

leh-*pol*

back

le dos

ler doh

toes

les doigts de pied

leh dwah der pee-*eh*

What a sight!
Quel spectacle!
kel spec*takl'*

What a mess!
Quel désastre
kel deh-*sastr'*

What a smell!
Quelle odeur!
kel oh-*der*

powder
la poudre
lah poodr'

baby
le bébé
ler beh-*beh*

perfume
le parfum
ler par*fuh*

story
l'histoire
leest*wah*

bedroom
la chambre
lah shombr'

bathroom
la salle de bain
lah sal der bah

A simple guide to pronouncing this French story

Dépêche-toi, Molly
dep-esh twah, moll*ee*

"Allez Molly, dans la salle de bain.
all*eh* moll*ee*, doh lah sal der bah

Ensuite je te raconterai une histoire", dit papa.
on*sweet* sher ter rakon-ter*eh* oon eest*wah*, dee pap-*ah*

"Porte-moi, porte-moi!"
port mwah, port mwah

Papa prend Molly dans ses bras.
pap-*ah* proh moll*ee* doh seh brah

"La tête en bas?"
lah tet oh bah

"Sur mon épaule?"
s'yoor moh eh-*pol*

"Ou sur mon dos?" demande papa.
oo s'yoor moh doh, d'*mond* pap-*ah*

"Comme un bébé!" dit Molly en riant.
kom ahn beh-*beh*, dee moll*ee* oh ree-*oh*

"Dépêche-toi, Molly," dit papa,
dep-esh twah, moll*ee*, dee pap-*ah*

"Je vais t'attendre dans ta chambre,"
sher veh tat-*ondr'* doh tah shombr'

"Lave-toi la figure," crie-t-il
lav twah lah feeg-*yoor*, creet*eel*

"et derrière les oreilles."
eh derry-*air* leh zor*ay*

"Lave-toi les dents."
lav twah leh doh

Molly se brosse aussi les cheveux...
moll*ee* ser bross oh-*see* leh sher-*ver*

à la gauche...
ah lah gosh

...à la droite,
ah lah drwaht

...sur son nez,
s'yoor soh neh

et le tout sur le haut de sa tête!
eh ler too s'yoor ler oh der sah tet

Molly se regarde dans le miroir de papa.
moll*ee* ser rer-*gard* doh ler meer*wah* der pap-*ah*

Son menton est long,
soh mont*oh* eh long

...ses yeux sont gros,
sez yer soh groh

...ses joues sont rondes.
seh shoo soh rond

Quel spectacle!
kel spec*takl'*

Elle se met de la poudre dans la main
el meh der lah poodr' doh sah mah

et elle souffle...
eh el soofl'

...et elle souffle!
eh el soofl'

Quel désastre!
kel deh-*sastr'*

Elle se met du parfum dans le cou...
el ser meh dew par*fuh* doh ler coo

...et sur ses doigts de pied.
eh s'yoor leh dwah der pee-*eh*

Quelle odeur!
kel oh-*der*

Soudain, Molly se souvient de son papa.
sood*ah* moll*ee* ser soovee*yah* der soh pap-*ah*

"J'arrive papa!" crie-t-elle.
shah-*reev* pap-*ah*, cree-*tel*

Mais devine ce que Molly trouve
meh der-*veen* ser ker moll*ee* troov

dans sa chambre?
doh sah shombr'

"Papa, réveille-toi! Je veux une histoire!"
pap-*ah*, reh-*vay* twah; sher verz oon eest*wah*

Mais il dort profondement et il ronfle!
meh eel dor profond'*moh* eh eel ronfl'